ANTSY AGATHA

By
Jennifer Langston

Illustrated by
i Cenizal

Tellwell Talent
www.tellwell.ca

ISBN
978-0-2288-4900-1 (Paperback)

My name is Agatha and sometimes I can't sit still.

My parents get mad and say "Agatha you need to chill!"

Chill, I try to do but get easily distracted.

It happens most when I see things that are attractive.

I start my chores but I don't
follow through.

I don't know why I don't complete them.
I know what to do!

The same thing happens all day in school.

I really try hard but sometimes I forget the rules.

A moment doing schoolwork can feel like hours.

I would ban school forever if I had the power!

When I am told to raise my hand,

I blurt out the answer... No one seems to understand.

Other kids tell me to wait my turn.

Waiting is hard to do, I don't know if I'll ever learn!

One day the teacher sent me home with a note.

Oh, no! I'm in trouble again.

My parents are going to tell me no TV... let me hide the remote!

When my parents read the note and to my surprise, I wasn't in trouble!

They said to me, we are going to get you some help because of your struggles.

"Struggles?" I asked, "What does that mean?"

They said, "We see you trying hard to do the right thing."

"We think it's best if we go see a therapist to get you some additional help."

"Mom and Dad... A therapist?" I said with a big yelp.

My parents laughed and said, "Let's try it and see."

I replied... "OK"... because it's not up to me.

We went to see the therapist and she made me feel good.

She listened to everything I said and really understood.

She called my parents back in the room and told us I had Attention Deficit Hyperactivity Disorder.

She then asked me, "Do you know what that is?" I lied and replied... "Kinda sorta."

She explained what it meant and that all my symptoms matched to the tee.

I said, "Uhm I still don't get it, could you break it down for me?"

She told me I have an awesome mind like that of a race car.

I said, "Yea like a race car that goes really far!"

She asked, "Does it go too fast sometimes?"

I said, "Yea how did you know? Wait, can you read my mind?"

She laughed and said, "No but I have many clients like you."

"Do you have trouble paying attention in school?"

I said, "Yes all the time and I feel like a fool."

She stated, "You're no fool, your mind is zooming all over the place bursting with new ideas."

My parents said, "Yea and It's been this way for years!"

I eagerly asked, "Can we do anything to fix it? Can we make a deal?

In order to go on my field trip, my teachers told me while I'm in class,

I must sit still."

My therapist smiled and said,

"First let's start by putting on the brakes to your race car brain."

I yelled, "Teach me because it's driving me insane!"

She said, "We don't use that word in here, but there are some things we can do.

We will need everyone on board, even your teachers too."

"Let's start by meeting once a week.

That will be a good start in helping you get what you seek."

We all agreed to meet every Friday and didn't change the day.

Every time we meet it seems like all we do is play.

She helps me with self-control and even my self-esteem.

I felt better about myself, and with pride I beam!

I was able to finally clean my room and focus on one thing at a time.

If I start to get distracted, my parents are there to encourage and tell me "You're doing fine!"

Therapy helps us all and improves how we relate.

My teachers notice a difference in class and are amazed at how much I participate.

Although, I still have trouble here and there,

I know that I can get help when I go to therapy and share.

So, if you can relate to anything I've said in this book...

Go see a therapist to get a second look.

You can make progress just like I did.

I even made a new friend; her name is Syd.

I went on my field trip and had a good time.

I sat still for an hour bus ride.

This is my story about how therapy helped my ADHD.

Antsy Agatha...that's me!

CPSIA information can be obtained
at www.ICGtesting.com
Printed in the USA
BVHW021402221121
622229BV00017B/614